Wild Weather

Written by Chris Oxlade

Contents

Collins

What is wild weather?

Wild weather is weather that is very windy, cold, hot, wet or dry. What's the wildest weather you've ever seen? Have you been blown about by super-strong winds? Have you been soaked to the skin by pouring rain? Have you heard thunder crashing right above your head?

The weather is sometimes so wild that it's better to stay indoors to keep safe. Floods, lightning, strong winds, hurricanes and tornadoes can often kill or injure people, destroy homes, or sink ships.

This book will take you on a journey around the Earth to see some of its wildest weather, finding out why it happens and where it takes place. We'll start with the coldest places of all – Antarctica and the Arctic ...

Coldest and snowiest

Even in the middle of summer, people in Antarctica and the Arctic have to wear a thick coat, hat and gloves! During winter, the temperature in Antarctica can fall as low as minus 80 degrees Celsius. It's almost as cold in the Arctic – around minus 65 degrees Celsius in the winter.

In the Antarctic summer, the Sun never sets. Even so, the temperature stays below freezing point (0 degrees Celsius), and the ground is always covered with snow and ice.

Frostbite

These freezing temperatures are cold enough to make uncovered fingers, toes and noses freeze within minutes which can cause frostbite. This can damage skin, and in extreme cases it can turn black and die.

Emperor penguins live on the ice in Antarctica.

COLD RECORD

In 1983, scientists at the Russian Vostok Station in Antarctica recorded a temperature of minus 89.2 degrees Celsius! That's the coldest temperature ever known on Earth.

Blizzards

It's very cold in other places, too. In Canada, just south of the Arctic, the temperature can fall to minus 40 degrees Celsius in winter. A mixture of snow and wind creates another type of wild weather, called a blizzard. During a blizzard, snow can reach a depth of more than a metre in just a few hours. This means that it quickly blocks roads, railways and airport runways. It can also pull down power lines and bury cars.

Mountain weather

The tops of high mountains are also freezing cold, snowy and windy. **Mountaineers** need warm clothes to climb high mountains, even when it's warm and sunny at the bottom.

THE DEEPEST SNOW

The snowiest place on Earth is Sukayu Onsen, in the mountains of Japan. On average, it gets an amazing 17.6 metres of snow each year! That's the same height as a five-storey building!

Hottest and driest

Many parts of the Earth get very hot, too. They are places on and close to the **equator** – an imaginary line around the middle of the Earth. This is where the Sun shines strongest.

There are many **deserts** close to the equator. The Sahara is a huge desert that stretches right across North Africa, north of the equator. People living in the Sahara have to protect themselves from the heat. They wear loose, light-coloured clothes that keep off the Sun's rays, but let air circulate to keep them cool.

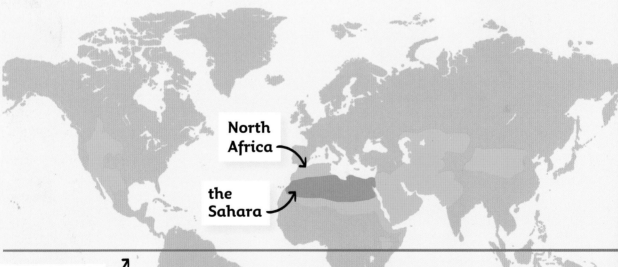

North Africa

the Sahara

the Equator

the Sahara Desert

TOP TEMPERATURE

The highest temperature ever recorded on Earth was a scorching 56.7 degrees Celsius, in Death Valley, California, in 1913.

Dry deserts

The hottest places can also be the driest. In some deserts it rains only a few times each year, and sometimes not for years on end.

Drought

Sometimes there's no rain for weeks or months in a place where it normally does rain. This is called a **drought**. The soil becomes dry and cracked, and crops and other plants die. This can leave people and animals without food.

Sandstorms and dust storms

In deserts, there's also another type of wild weather: sandstorms. Strong, swirling winds blow sand into the air, covering everything in dust and making it difficult for people and animals to breathe. Dust storms can also happen when there's a **drought**. The dry soil is blown into the air, taking it away from the crops and causing problems for farmers.

THE DRIEST PLACE

The world's driest place is the Atacama Desert, in South America. In some parts of the Atacama, not a single drop of rain has ever been recorded!

Rain and more rain

Unlike deserts, many places get a lot of rain. The steamy Amazon rainforest is one of the wettest places on the planet. Here it rains almost every day, and plants love the warm, wet weather that helps them to grow.

Monsoon rains

In many places around the world, but mainly in Asia, there are both dry seasons and wet seasons during the year. The wet season is called the **monsoon**. For a few months, thick clouds roll in from the sea, bringing heavy rain almost every day.

THE WETTEST PLACE

The town of Mawsynram in northern India gets heavy monsoon rains. An amazing 11.9 metres of rain falls here every year — enough to drown a three-storey house!

Motorcyclists hold up umbrellas to shelter from the monsoon rains.

Floods

When heavy rain falls every day, as it does during a monsoon, streams and rivers can't carry away the rainwater fast enough. The rivers fill up and then overflow, and water floods the land alongside the rivers. This means that farmland, villages and towns can be under water, sometimes for weeks or months, ruining crops and homes.

SOMERSET FLOODS

In late 2013 and early 2014, a record amount of rainfall fell in southern England. A low-lying area of land called the Somerset levels was badly flooded, and hundreds of people had to leave their homes. The water took months to drain away.

FLASH FLOODS

Flash floods happen when it rains extremely heavily in one place. The streets can be dry one minute, but deep under water a few minutes later. The rain water can flow very fast, bursting into homes and washing away cars.

Thunder and lightning

Heavy rain is often accompanied by thunderstorms. Thunderstorms happen every day in the tropics, the area around the middle of the Earth. Thunderstorms are created by thunderclouds which start small but grow taller and taller and wider and wider. A fully-grown thundercloud, called a cumulonimbus cloud, is about 10 kilometres high.

Cumulonimbus cloud

You can recognise a thundercloud from far away because its top is spread out.

This car is covered with hailstones after a storm.

Super-strong winds blow up and down inside a thundercloud, carrying water drops and **ice crystals** up and down. The drops and crystals grow bigger and bigger until they hurtle to the ground. Hailstones sometimes fall from thunderclouds.

AFRICAN STORMS

More thunderstorms happen in Africa than anywhere else in the world. You can hear the rumble of thunder and see flashes of lightning almost every day of the year.

Lightning

The streak of lightning you see during a thunderstorm is a giant spark of electricity. Ice crystals or raindrops bump into each other inside a thunder cloud. This makes positive electric charges and negative electric charges build inside the cloud. The electric charges in the cloud make charges build up in the ground, too. When the positive and negative charges get very large, a spark jumps between them with a flash.

Lightning makes thunder

As lightning jumps through the air, it heats the air very quickly. This makes the air expand suddenly, which makes the boom that we hear as thunder.

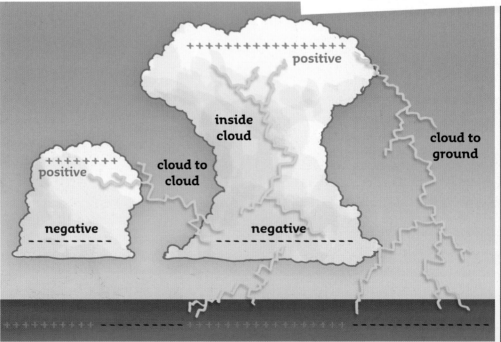

How lightning is formed

THE MOST LIGHTNING STRIKES

The place that gets the most lightning strikes is the Catatumbo River in Venezuela. On average it has 3,600 lightning strikes in an hour!

Tornadoes

The biggest thunderstorms create tornadoes. A tornado is a spinning column of air, shaped like a giant funnel. Tornadoes are sometimes called twisters because of the way they look. Tornadoes bring the world's strongest winds. Tornadoes happen all over the world, but some places get lots of them. Tornado Alley, in the USA, got its name because hundreds of tornadoes hit the area every year.

How a tornado is formed

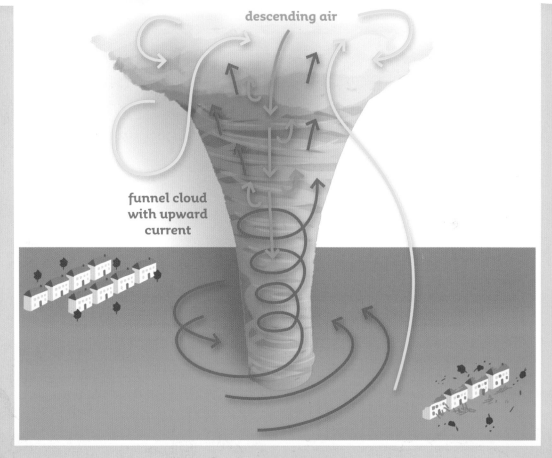

descending air

funnel cloud with upward current

Touchdown

If the bottom end of a tornado touches the ground, the violent winds smash everything to pieces. The wind picks up anything in its path – trees, fences, houses – and hurls them around and around. In 1931, in Mississippi, a tornado even picked up a heavy train and threw it 30 metres through the air!

TORNADO RECORD

The fastest wind ever measured was in a tornado — blowing at 484 kilometres per hour. That's as fast as the world's fastest express train.

A tornado in Oklahoma

On 20 May 2013 at 3:57 in the afternoon, a tornado touched down near the city of Moore, near Oklahoma City, USA. It was a giant, growing until it was an incredible 2.1 kilometres wide. Inside, winds reached a terrifying 340 kilometres per hour. The tornado lasted for 39 minutes and travelled for 27 kilometres.

The tornado demolished a road bridge, farm buildings and factories. It destroyed 1,150 homes, a primary school and threw a car up on to the roof of a medical centre. Sadly, 24 people were killed and 377 injured.

tornado damage in Oklahoma

Hurricanes

Just like a tornado, a hurricane is made up of swirling cloud. The winds in a hurricane aren't as strong as they are in a tornado, but a hurricane is hundreds or thousands of times bigger. Hurricanes bring the most powerful and extreme weather on Earth. They grow from groups of thunderstorms that move slowly across the sea, gaining energy. Hurricanes are also sometimes called typhoons or cyclones.

How a hurricane is formed

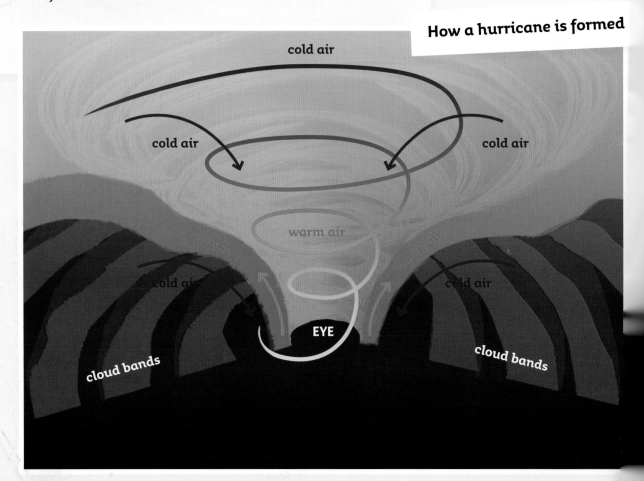

cold air

cold air

cold air

warm air

cold air

cold air

EYE

cloud bands

cloud bands

Inside a hurricane

A hurricane contains thick bands of cloud and a clear hole in the centre, called the eye. Hurricanes bring super-strong winds, heavy rain and thunderstorms. They can also push up giant waves at sea. When the waves hit the coast, they pour inland and flood everything in their path.

THE LARGEST HURRICANE

The biggest hurricane ever recorded was called Typhoon Tip and formed in the Pacific Ocean in 1979. It grew to 2,220 kilometres across.

Hurricane Katrina

In most years, a hurricane hits the south-east coast of the USA, damaging property and taking lives. In August 2009, a hurricane grew over the Atlantic Ocean and started to move towards the USA. Each new hurricane is given a name, and this one was called Katrina. On 29 August, it hit the coast of Louisiana, close to the city of New Orleans.

Hurricane Katrina's strong winds pushed sea water on to the coasts, causing extreme flooding. New Orleans was protected by flood barriers, but Katrina pushed the sea level up so high that water poured over the barriers and into the city. In some places the water grew to six metres deep.

About 1,800 people died because of Hurricane Katrina. Most of them were trapped in their houses in New Orleans and drowned. It was a terrible disaster. The city is still recovering from it, and many people have never returned to their damaged homes.

a fishing boat wrecked by hurricane Katrina

North America

Path of Hurricane Katrina

Atlantic Ocean

South America

path of Hurricane Katrina

The hurricane damaged many people's houses.

Take cover!

We've seen that the Earth's weather can be very wild indeed, but how can we protect ourselves from it? Sometimes we just need to wear the right clothes. But for some wild weather, such as tornadoes, special shelters are used to protect people and animals.

Predicting wild weather

One way of protecting ourselves is to **forecast** when wild weather such as blizzards and floods might happen. Then people have a chance to get away before the wild weather strikes. Powerful computers are helping weather experts to get better at forecasting all the time.

Future weather

Many weather scientists think that we'll get more wild weather in the future, because of **global warming** and **climate change**. This means it's extremely important for us all to do everything we can to prevent climate change, as well as being more prepared than ever for wild weather.

Glossary

climate change
change in the pattern of weather around the world that many scientists believe is due to global warming

deserts
dry, often sandy regions that don't get much rain

drought
long period of very dry weather

equator
imaginary line around the middle of the earth, an equal distance from both the South Pole and the North Pole

forecast
prediction of what the weather will be like over the next few hours, days or weeks

global warming
slow increase in the overall temperature of the earth's atmosphere

ice crystals
small crystals of solid ice that grow inside a cloud

monsoon
period of heavy rains

mountaineers
people who climb mountains

storey
one level of a building

Index

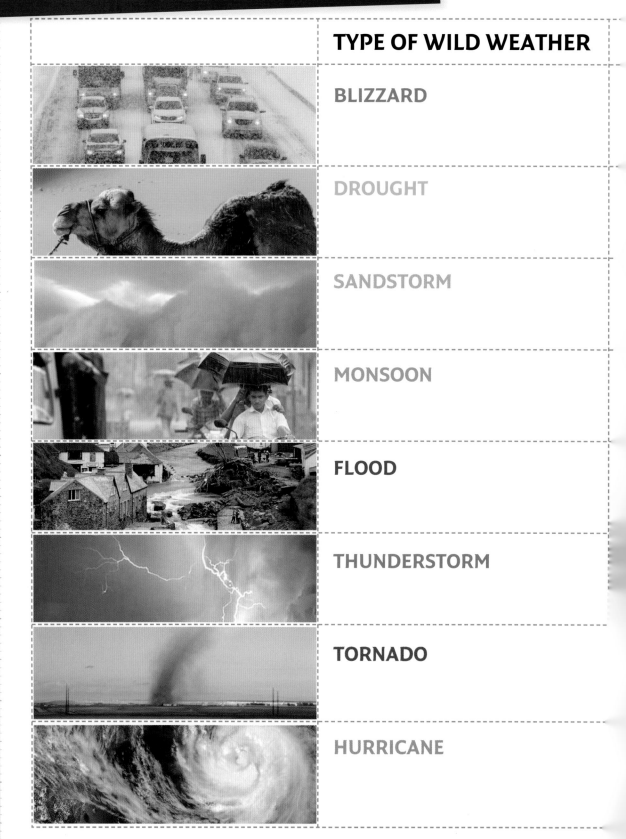

	TYPE OF WILD WEATHER
	BLIZZARD
	DROUGHT
	SANDSTORM
	MONSOON
	FLOOD
	THUNDERSTORM
	TORNADO
	HURRICANE

WHERE DOES IT HAPPEN?	WHAT CAUSES IT?
Where there are cold winters and on mountain tops	Heavy snow and strong winds at the same time
Where there is normally only a small amount of rain	The rains fail to fall, so the ground dries up
In deserts	Strong winds blow sand or dust into the air
In tropical parts of the world, particularly in Asia	Winds
In almost any part of the world, apart from the Arctic and Antarctica	Rain falling for a long time, or a burst of very heavy rain
Mostly in the tropics	Electricity building up inside enormous clouds
In many places, but mostly in the centre of the USA	Violent winds inside a massive thunderstorm
In the Atlantic, Pacific and Indian Oceans	Thunderstorms turning into a vast, swirling storm

Ideas for reading

Written by Clare Dowdall, PhD

Lecturer and Primary Literacy Consultant

Learning objectives: read aloud books closely matched to improving phonic knowledge, sounding out unfamiliar words accurately, automatically and without undue hesitation; answer and ask questions; explain and discuss understanding of books, poems and other material, both those that they listen to and those that they read for themselves; participate in discussions, presentations, performances and debates

Curriculum links: Geography

Interest words: climate change, deserts, drought, equator, forecast, global warming, ice crystals, monsoon, mountaineers, storey, blizzard, tornado, hurricane

Word count: 1181

Resources: pens and paper, ICT resources, globe or atlas

Getting started

- Look at the front cover together. Ask children to share their experiences of being in wild weather.

- Read the blurb with the children. Notice how wild weather is described using noun phrases.

- Turn to the contents page. Ask children to suggest where in the world each type of wild weather may happen.

Reading and responding

- Read pp 2–5 with the children. Challenge children to retrieve key facts from pp 4–5, by asking questions, e.g. which parts of the body are at the most risk from the cold? Model how to scan the text for key words to answer the question.

- Practise reading long and less familiar words, using sounding out and blending as a strategy, e.g. Vostok Station in Antarctica.

- Challenge children to read to p 28, noting some key facts about wild weather to share with the group later.

Returning to the book

- When children have finished reading, ask for key facts about wild weather. Ask children to show the page that contains their key fact(s) to encourage accurate fact retrieval.

- Turn to pp 30–31. Check that children can read the table by asking the some quick-fire questions. Locate each incident on the globe or map.

- Challenge children to work in pairs to find out the similarities and differences between hurricanes and tornadoes. Support their use of the contents, and skimming and scanning techniques to locate and retrieve information.